A Nantucket Nanny

Limericks by **MOLLY MANLEY**

Illustrations by **JANET MARSHALL**

COMMONWEALTH EDITIONS
Beverly, Massachusetts

To William and Mollie and Papa Dick

M. M.

To my favorite Islanders,
Joan Craig
and
the late Grace Grossman

J. M.

ISBN-13: 978-1-889833-96-5
ISBN-10: 1-889833-96-7

Library of Congress Cataloging-in-Publication Data
Manley, Molly (Molly Hollingworth)
A Nantucket nanny : limericks / by Molly Manley ; illustrations by Janet Marshall.
p. cm.
ISBN 1-889833-96-7
1. Limericks. I. Marshall, Janet Perry. II. Title.
PN6231.L5M374 2005
811'.54—dc22
2005000212

Printed in China

Commonwealth Editions
266 Cabot Street, Beverly, Massachusetts 01915
www.commonwealtheditions.com

A Nantucket nanny, Miss Peach,
Pedaled the twins to Cliff Beach.
They looked so alike
Strapped onto her bike,
She couldn't tell which twin was each!

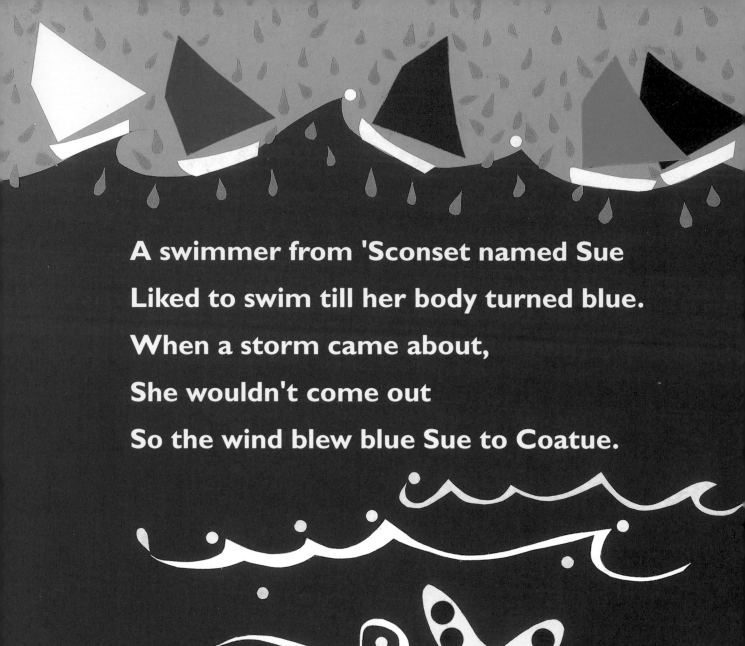

A swimmer from 'Sconset named Sue
Liked to swim till her body turned blue.
When a storm came about,
She wouldn't come out
So the wind blew blue Sue to Coatue.

Poor Georgie went out for a jog

But got lost in the Shawkemo fog.

The fog was so thick

He tripped on a stick

And fell into a cranberry bog.

CRANBERRIES

A Pocomo artist of note

Made his home on a tippy old boat.

When the ocean got choppy

His palette got sloppy

And splatted all over his coat.

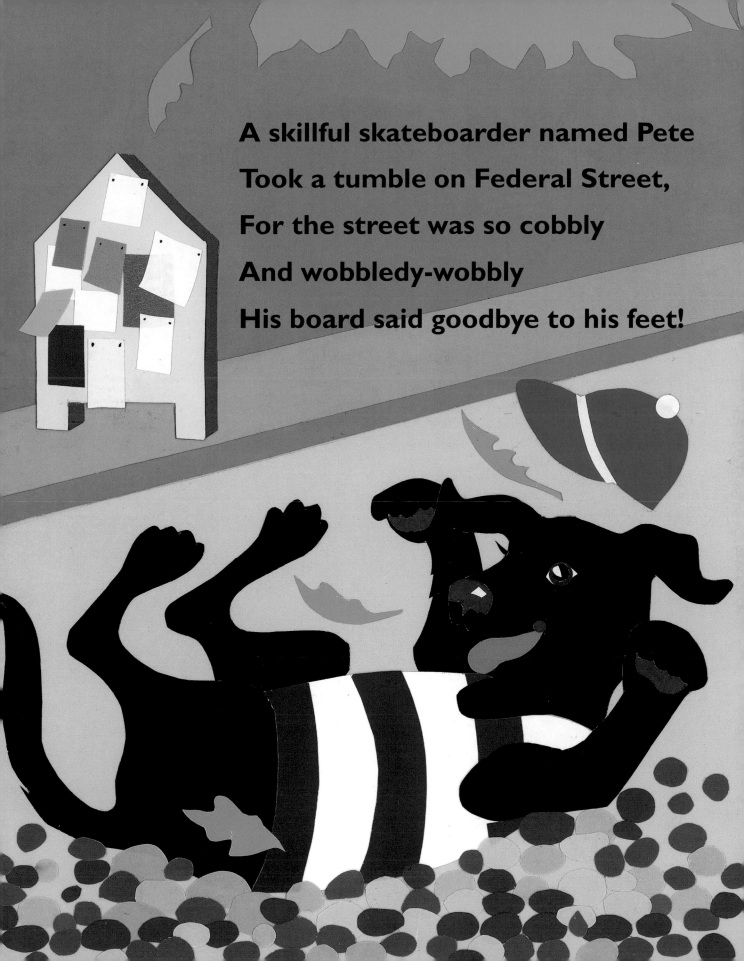

A skillful skateboarder named Pete

Took a tumble on Federal Street,

For the street was so cobbly

And wobbledy-wobbly

His board said goodbye to his feet!

Beneath the town wharf at low tide

A mischievous crew likes to hide.

They munch on junk food

And float in the nude

As they chew with their mouths open wide.

A sailor from Cisco called Kerrie

Decided to race the Fast Ferry.

She heeled with great style

For a nautical mile

While everyone clowned and made merry.

A triplet from Quidnet named Lizzy
Made her sisters so mad they got dizzy.
She'd snivel and pout
And refuse to go out
For her hair was impossibly frizzy.

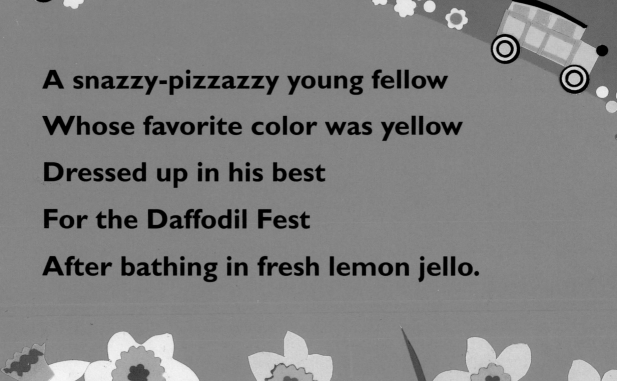

A snazzy-pizzazzy young fellow

Whose favorite color was yellow

Dressed up in his best

For the Daffodil Fest

After bathing in fresh lemon jello.

A sweetheart from Tuckernuck Isle,

Admired for her sunshiny smile,

Ate nothing but sweets

And scandalous treats

Till her teeth tumbled out in a pile.

A fun-loving nipper, Annette,

Rode the shuttle to old Madaket.

She sang salty tunes

As she slid down the dunes,

Saluting the famous sunset.

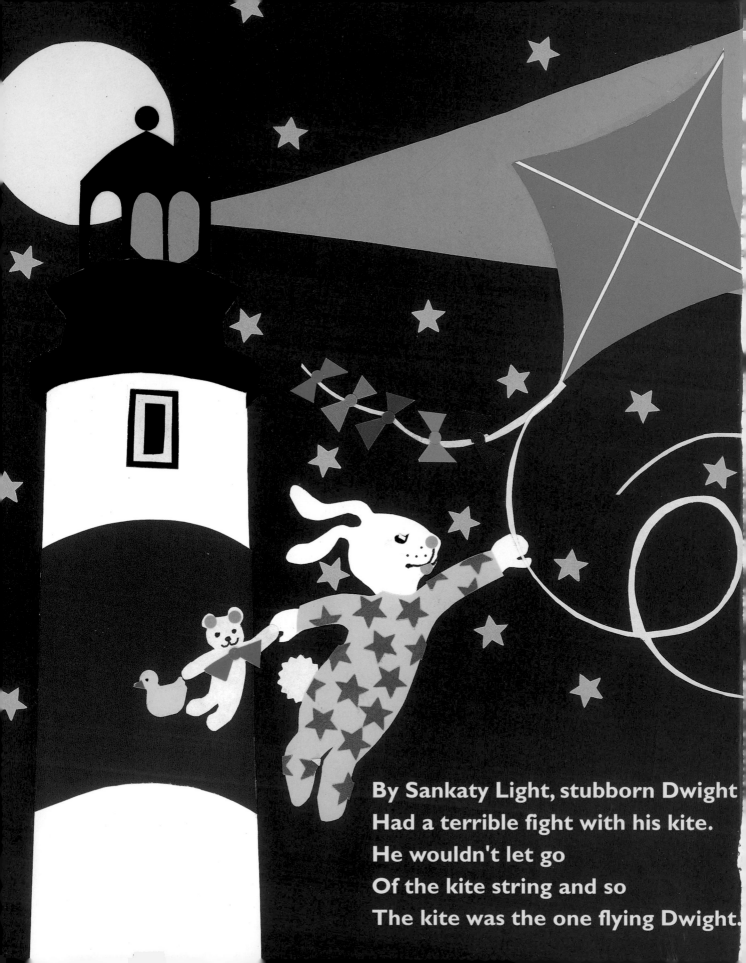

By Sankaty Light, stubborn Dwight
Had a terrible fight with his kite.
He wouldn't let go
Of the kite string and so
The kite was the one flying Dwight.